RAIN IN THE TOWN

ACHYUT PRASHAST SINGH

ISBN 979-888591530-4

ABOUT THE BOOK

Rain in the Town, at core, is a story about two things: love and violence. The story can be best described as a romantic action thriller, which follows a lovelorn man and the violent journey he undertakes due to this "love". All the bloodshed, battles and pain are caused by love at core, be it its abundance or scarcity. The protagonist is a flawed man, and there are times I have played with his characterization to surprise the viewers. I wanted this story to cover at least 12 chapters, the way many anime shows often have 12 episodes in their first seasons. However, I realized the story was done in just 10 chapters, and dragging or extending anymore would simply be overkill. A lot of people prefer reading short stories, so this book, I hope, can work for them.

This is a story about love, and also about loss and pain. A lot of people go through these stages. Of course, not everyone goes out wielding a sword and killing people in the way, but that's what fiction is for, isn't it? I was going to kill some characters in what you might prefer calling surprise twists, but I knew it would again be overkill. And so, I have left the first draft of the story untouched. Yes, what you are about to read is the first and final draft of this story. I can't recommend it for kids, since it is full of violence and intensity not targeted at them, even if they're used to violence in movies and TV shows. Plus, its themes at core are mature and require a developed mindset to be fully understood and accepted.

I thank you for buying this copy and it genuinely makes me happy to have been chosen to provide you with a story that can captivate you as you go on to read it. Thanks a lot!

- Achyut Prashast Singh, the author

Contents

CHAPTER ONE

"A heart that loves is the one that gives,
This is how everyone who loves someone lives.
It's not about what and how much you receive,
Love is a magic that does not deceive."

This is the story of Naresh. He was a total outcast, hated by many. His fault? Being the son of a man accused of harassment. This did impact his relationship with his father who often thought he could never redeem himself. This only added fuel to the fire, as Naresh never looked up to his father or thought about how to help him. His father, named Atul, always knew it that he was falsely accused of harassment and that he could fight off such accusations, but simply didn't since his wife's death left him and his son alone. Naresh didn't really know whether or not he was the culprit. He just wanted to live his life and fulfill his dreams. The society, however, was not willing to forgive Atul and in the process made Naresh suffer for years. He developed a low self-esteem, becoming anxious and depressed. His friends left him one-by-one, and there was no one to console him or stand by him.

One day, however, when he was crying while eating his cold sandwiches at college, a girl dared to talk to him. She came for him, and asked him if he was alright. Naresh had always been shy and nervous, and to see a girl smile at him and ask about his condition was an extremely exciting yet frightening experience for him. She said she heard him cry and couldn't bear hearing him like that. She offered him a handkerchief and gave another beautiful smile that made Naresh's heart melt. He finally drummed up the courage to ask her name, which was revealed as Aastha. And thus they began meeting during lunch time every day. One day, Aastha decided to switch lunches with Naresh, who initially advised against it, believing his food to be too cold and tasteless. However, Aastha let him eat her lunch and happily ate his cold sandwiches. This gesture by her made Naresh develop feelings for her. He was already "breathtaken" by her gorgeous looks, but seeing these humane qualities in her made him fall for her as they kept on meeting and strengthening their bonds.

He was left heartbroken when another boy proposed to her and she reciprocated. Naresh was an outcast once again, and Aastha never met him after that day. Naresh had carefully selected the best flowers he could as a gift for her. It was all in vain and Naresh was in pain. He kept getting bullied and ridiculed by his classmates, and that only made him lonelier. He had no one left to talk to, share his feelings with or hang out with. Naresh decided to put an end to this misery and decided to stop expecting love or warmth from those around him. Securing excellent grades in the final exams, he topped the college and only the teachers congratulated him, while everyone else just made fun of him or accused him of cheating somehow.

Naresh was about to go away, before Aastha showed up to congratulate him. Naresh felt the warmth and thanked her for the wishes. However, Aastha's boyfriend Nikhil acted hostile towards him upon seeing the two shake hands. He asked Aastha if Naresh was her brother, and she kept saying "just a good friend", but Naresh himself started to feel enraged. He calmly told him he's not her brother but just a friend... an old friend. Seeing him talk back, Nikhil punched him and broke his nose. As everyone gathered upon seeing this, Naresh found his rage uncontrollable and delivered a heavy blow to his face as well. A fight ensued between the two, with Naresh repeating he's not Aastha's brother and continuing to beat Nikhil black and blue. This is where Aastha intervened, grabbed Naresh's shirt and gave him a tight slap for "murderously" beating Nikhil up. Naresh first found his anger uncontrollable, and now his tears. Aastha angrily looked at him and picking up an injured Nikhil told him, *"You don't deserve anyone, freak."* Naresh was left looking around, finding the crowd quietly staring at him. This is when Nikhil pushed Aastha away and delivered a tooth-breaking kick to Naresh's face, damaging one of his frontal teeth by half.

Naresh grabbed his prizes and ran away from the college. Entering a subway station's washroom, he quickly and quietly washed the blood and injuries in his mouth and boarded the train back to home. During the commute, he felt numb. He heard a co-passenger talk to his friend about drinking to get rid of pain. Naresh almost felt convinced to drink for the first time in life since his pain had gotten worse. However, he quickly told himself it's not a good thing and continued to exit the train upon arriving at his station. He walked towards home, and as a few good-looking girls walked past him, he felt happy as well as worried that he might be seen as creepy for merely looking at them. Arriving home, he heard gunshots inside. He threw his bag aside and rushed inside to see what was going on. He found himself surrounded by a pile of corpses stabbed with knives and other sharp objects. He entered one of the rooms and saw his father sitting in the balcony, probably breathing his last.

Naresh rushed towards Atul who acted as if nothing happened at all. He only had this much to say to his son:

"It's settled. The dispute I had with the society is now permanently settled. I don't have anything to prove to anyone, but you, my son, must know that I never harassed any woman in life. As for these men lying dead in our house... they came for you. I had no problem with them, until they said they would hack you to death, I couldn't resist killing them. I wanted to protect you. Listen, son. I don't have much time left, so keep listening to my words. As a husband, I failed big time, but I don't want to fail as a father, even if I end up actually failing. I love you, son. I only have a simple advice for you: work hard, fulfill your dreams, get a job, find a woman, and live a good life with her till death. Who knows what happens after dying...

The funny part is, I will find it out now but won't ever be able to tell you about that. Dark comedy in real life is either really bad... or just simply hilarious."

Naresh tearfully smiled and hugged Atul, only to see him pass away in a few seconds. He began crying and kept hugging his father's corpse. In a few hours, the cops came but found only the corpses of the attackers and Atul. Naresh ran away with the determination to return, clear his father's name and achieve the goals set for him. Thus began a boy's journey towards becoming a man: one who would die as much as he would kill for the one thing everyone in this world wants: love.

"No matter how much pain it endures,
Even if loving it is forsaken.
A loving heart will always win,
And find itself in love breathtaken."

CHAPTER TWO

"A heart is wandering here and there,
After abandoning its tragic past.
It believes it has finally found peace,
But doesn't know how long it will last."

Naresh runs away and arrives at a point where he must determine whether or not to live the life he had always been living. Remembering his father's advice, he tells himself to work hard first to fulfill his dreams of becoming a swordsman. He collects money from his father's account and joins a club that teaches him martial arts and swordsmanship. In the meanwhile, he also picks up a part-time job as a pizza deliveryman. He works hard for several months and finally becomes a skilled swordsman. However, he only wants to use it as a skill and not as a full-time sports profession. His dream has been fulfilled, and now he needs to find a job.

Unlike other men of his age who have support from various sources, Naresh has none. He doesn't have any friends, and a girlfriend? Absolutely none. Naresh has told himself to never fall in love after that incident with Aastha. In order to help himself follow the order, he has been lying to himself that he never had feelings for Aastha. He suppresses his romantic feelings towards any girl he happens to like. This leads to trouble as he grows up. Two years pass, and he has found a full-time job at the local news agency. He has still suppressed his romantic feelings in spite of knowing that bottling emotions will only make things worse. He believes he doesn't need a girl to love him back, and decides to never marry as well.

Things start to change with the arrival of a new neighbor. Her name is Sunanda, and she instantly notices Naresh and his introverted nature in a few days. One night, she knocks at his door and offers him some special kind of noodles to eat. Naresh acts as if he is happy and accepts the noodles. Before going to bed, he looks at himself in the mirror and begins smiling. His smile only gets bigger when he tells himself he couldn't resist looking at her pretty face. He also reminds himself that even though he has planned never to fall in love or get married, sweet girls like her can make him change his decision anytime.

Few more weeks later, when Naresh and Sunanda have become friends, things change. Naresh has now fallen for Sunanda and expresses these feelings deeply while talking to himself. He starts tearing up with the realization that maybe he has finally found a woman who can accept and love him, and also that a woman might not really find a man like him "strong enough": to love. These mixed-up emotions begin to cause turmoil and keep making Naresh shyer while looking at any kind of good-looking women. He experiences warmth and excitement at the same time, but with Sunanda around, he only feels better.

Naresh and Sunanda have now become more than just friends. Naresh wants to express his emotions, and asks Sunanda out. She happily agrees and the two visit a coffee shop. Naresh, while talking about the relationship, ends up being vulnerable with Sunanda as he says this:

"I-I don't know how to say this. I had told myself to never fall in love again after one debacle. I even lied to myself; I kept

telling myself I had no feelings for her, while I clearly knew I did have feelings for. Nevertheless, meeting you made me realize I can't help falling for a girl I like. I really like you, Sunanda. I have been breathtaken ever since I saw you. Your qualities only made you more and more likable. I know that I'm not a perfect man, and that I have my weaknesses, but I am willing to change and work towards becoming a better person. I have never told this to anyone but I suffer from an anxiety order. It's your right to know this beforehand so that you don't feel cheated later on. Oh no... I am ruining any chances of ending up with you by saying all this. But this... all of this matters. Because in short... I love you."

Sunanda feels moved by his words. Seeing him vulnerable like that leaves her convinced. She smiles and reciprocates. Naresh finds this so unbelievable that he is left crying. Sunanda hugs him and this makes Naresh happier. Everyone in the coffee shop claps for the two, and the shy Naresh jumps in excitement. He has finally found his woman, and now he has to live a happy life with her forever.

Naresh thinks his mission is close to completion, but then something changes his life forever.

He reminds himself he has to clear his father's name from the false accusations. When he talks to Sunanda about it, she decides to help him. However, he has no evidence to prove his father was innocent. He visits the city he left once again, with some hope, and is treated with contempt. Sunanda is also told to leave Naresh due to his father's reputation. Just when Naresh starts asking people politely, another man arrives in the city and brings along evidence against Atul.

Naresh is shocked to see the footage of his father killing men and actually harassing women. Sunanda looks at him with shock and continues to watch the disturbing video. Naresh grabs the man by his collar and asks him how he found the videos and who recorded them. The man, named Deepak, tells him he himself filmed the videos. Naresh tries to tell everyone something is wrong with the videos, but doesn't have the courage to. Sunanda is left devastated and is further taunted for loving him. Naresh tries to tell her he has nothing to do with any of this, but Sunanda begins tearing up and leaves him.

Naresh stands in front of his former home, and asks himself if trusting his father in his final times was a right decision. He becomes depressed once again, and wants to blame Sunanda for not trusting him, but also realizes any other girl would possibly do that. He decides to find out the truth behind the videos on one hand, but also wants to let go of his past on the other. He begins tearing up and looks at the sky, wondering if he will ever get rid of his father's image and find the love he needs, if not deserves. Naresh decides to cut ties with his father's image and live responsibly. He returns home, and thanks to Sunanda, everyone now knows that Naresh is the son of a violent criminal.

Naresh ends up losing his job, and enraged, he meets Sunanda at her home. She doesn't allow him to enter, but he forcefully enters and slaps her in a fit of rage.

"*Wow, you're no better than your criminal father.*" says Sunanda.

Naresh realizes what he has done, and tearfully apologizes. Sunanda begins crying as well. Naresh then gets up and walks out of her house. He feels the urge to drink for the first time and let go of pain, but slaps himself, telling he deserves this suffering and that nothing should help him in this condition.

"A heart was mostly hated by other hearts,
And was truly to the core shaken.
Then it found a loving heart
And in love was breathtaken."

CHAPTER THREE

"A lonely heart decided to move on,
After its only source of love was lost.
It might eventually find another source,
But doesn't know how much it will cost."

Two years later, Naresh, who is now living it another city, has returned home after a long time. He walks towards his flat and before entering, knocks on the door, only to insert the key and open it. He reacts as if his imaginary girlfriend has opened it and hugged him instantly. He enters the flat, closes the door, takes a shower and sits down to eat his breakfast. He keeps looking at the chair in front of him and pretends to be looking at "her". He smiles here and there in between and tells her to "stop" or else he might start blushing too. He washes the dishes and begins talking to the imaginary girlfriend:

"I have finally learned martial arts, baby. It was tough, but it felt good to learn something so enthusiastically. You'd have loved seeing me there. Come here and give me a kiss on the cheek... Thank you. I love you; truly and completely. You are always there when I want you and always with me while I'm awake or asleep. Thank you... Sandhya."

Yes. Naresh now has Sandhya, an imaginary girlfriend. He imagines any beautiful girl on the internet as her, and fantasizes about her as Sandhya. He goes to the movies, and imagines she would also want to see the same film. He goes to eat pizza, he imagines she would want to eat the same pizza as his. Every time, everywhere, Naresh finds himself accompanied by the imaginary girlfriend who doesn't doubt him, doesn't disturb him and always brings him happiness even without actually existing. Naresh is fully aware of this, but imagining being with a girl he likes gives him more pleasure than being alone would give him pain.

He is now living what he prefers to call a simple life. He plans to visit a hill station with the expectation of turning his imaginary girlfriend into a real one. He boards the train with a bag or two and goes to his seat. He listens to music and closes his eyes, imagining a new favorite actress as Sandhya, following which he slowly opens his eyes and smiles.

He then looks around himself and pulls out the earphones. With nobody looking except the passenger in front of him, he quickly draws out his sword and counters attack from a group of assassins. Everyone is shocked as the fight unfolds. While making sure no one else is hurt, Naresh gives the assassins a tough fight. He manages to get them near the door. Using a newly perfected move, he chops off all their hands and kicks them all out of the train at once. He then washes the blood on the sword and proceeds to return to his seat, only to realize a drop of blood is still on his face. Other passengers are now totally terrified of him.

Who are they and why did they come after him? Here's what happened before he was "learning martial arts" away from the city.

Naresh kept visiting his abandoned home and it brought back violent, depressing memories since he couldn't believe his father actually did it. He decided to sell the house and use the money somewhere. This is when he met Deepak once again. Yes, the same guy who filmed his father's videos of violence. As Deepak began teasing him about losing his faith in his father as well as the "only" girlfriend he had, it angered Naresh but he chose to remain quiet due to his father's actions. He had almost decided to leave quietly without saying a word, but the moment Deepak said that the videos "could be fake", Naresh grabbed him by the collar once again, which didn't go down well with Deepak, who kicked him away.

An enraged Naresh tried fighting back, only to be constantly kicked by Deepak who also kept taunting him about being a bad son and lover to Sunanda. Naresh was surprised as to how he knew Sunanda's name. Deepak revealed he loved Sunanda much before Naresh entered the scene. Being the son of an influential man, Deepak fell for Sunanda after she consoled him when his brother died. They became friends and their bond grew deeper when they first went on a date. Deepak proposed to her, and she instantly reciprocated. When Naresh asked what happened after that, Deepak stopped hitting him and told him it was a personal issue and he won't disclose it to a stranger. All he could disclose was that he still loved her, and that Naresh should no longer try to pursue her.

Following this, Naresh went straight to Sunanda's home and forced his entry. He asked her about why she "pretended" to love him if she already had a boyfriend. Sunanda expressed mixed feelings over this and said she didn't want to see him anymore. Naresh grew hostile and said he could kill Deepak, just to provoke her, but she smiled and told him to get some treatment for the injuries caused by Deepak. This made Naresh feel sadder and for the first time he felt disappointed about being physically weak. This is what prompted him to go and learn martial arts. He became skilled in handling different types of swords, even small knives. His training took a few years before he returned to his home once again. This time, he went to Deepak and asked him about the videos involving his father. Before Deepak could even touch him, Naresh dodged his blow and kicked him. Thus unfolded a short but effectively violent fistfight between the two, which ended with Naresh winning. He grabbed Deepak by the collar again, and delivered a heavy punch to his face. As Deepak collapsed, Sunanda came running out of the house to stop Naresh, who quickly pulled out his sword and pointed it at her without knowing it was her. He realized it was her the moment he turned in the direction of the sword. It began raining. Sunanda told him she was married to Deepak and that she still didn't want to see him. Naresh told her he would kill Deepak if he didn't reveal how he filmed his father killing people.

Deepak revealed the killings showcased in the video were real, except his father was forced to kill the people for money. "*Who forced him?*" asked Naresh. "*My dad.*" replied Deepak. Naresh was left surprised already, but the surprise doubled up when Sunanda said, "*Me too*".

"A heart that dared is now in trouble,
Everyone wants to burst its bubble.
Either there will be something remaining,
Or everything will turn to rubble."

CHAPTER FOUR

"A heart that loves is also enraged,
A war against everyone it has waged.
Its power is love and only love,
Which can neither be destroyed nor be caged."

Naresh stood surprised. Sunanda admitted she was also involved. This whole plan's mastermind was Deepak's father, Rajan, who wanted Atul, a part-time killer, to kill more targets even though the latter had retired from the killing business. Rajan was worried since one of his dying henchmen had told him there was a mole in his gang. This is where Sunanda entered and asked Atul to kill in exchange for having her as his son's bride. Atul, since he cared for Naresh and wanted him to be happily married, somehow agreed to make the killings. However, Rajan's plan was to kill every man in his gang since he was tired to trying to find who it was. This surprised Atul, since he didn't expect to kill this many people. Killing everyone also meant he was killing "innocents". Nevertheless, Atul grabbed the sword and killed every henchman. He was, however, shocked to secretly realize he had been filmed doing so.

He received his payment and went away, but worried about the footage. What if it ended up in the wrong hands? He needed to get rid of the footage somehow, even if it meant killing someone. In an attempt to snatch it, Atul disguised himself and attacked Deepak. However, with intervention from the guards, Atul failed to retrieve it and got caught. However, he somehow managed to flee the scene, albeit without the footage. Rajan became enraged to learn of this and decided to send his henchmen to kill Atul. The rest is history since the follow-up led to Atul's death and a final conversation with Naresh. However, Rajan was still puzzled when he realized the mole was not among his henchmen as the real mole obtained evidence against him and handed it over to the cops.

Rajan still believes the mole is alive, except he has become "dormant".

Hearing all of this, Naresh angrily asked Deepak about the videos where his father was seen harassing women and if they were real. Deepak revealed the videos were real.

This made Naresh feel it would be unfair if he killed Deepak just to defend Atul. But could Deepak be potentially lying? Possibly. Deepak began smiling as Naresh lowered his sword. Sunanda felt relieved. However, Rajan's henchmen arrived with their bladed weapons and surrounded Naresh. The rain intensified as Naresh closed his eyes for a few seconds and told himself:

"I am doing this for myself, my life. Not for you, dad."

Naresh quickly opened his eyes and began fighting the henchmen as Sunanda and Deepak stood there watching. A henchman tried to slash him with a sickle, but ended up losing his arm thanks to Naresh's sword. Another one lost a leg, while others kept losing more blood and limbs as well. After the rainwater on the ground turned red with blood, Naresh pointed the sword towards Deepak and went on to say this:

"Deepak! Thanks to that video of my father harassing women, I am a bit too ashamed to kill you. If I did, it would

haunt me and make it seem as if I assisted him. This sense of guilt... I don't want it. You and... your wife can live however you want. Do anything. It doesn't concern me anymore. I have lost belief in a number of things, and love seems to be among those. I can't say if I want to fall in love again because your wife clearly distracted and dumped me as a part of the game. Well, good for all three of us. I don't know what I did to deserve this kind of treatment, but I am giving you two a last chance. Stay away from me, and I'll stay away from you."

Naresh wiped the blood on his sword with the rainwater and proceeded to walk away as Rajan's henchmen continued to die due to excessive blood loss. Deepak felt enraged and pulled out his gun, but Sunanda stopped him from firing. She then gave him a kiss and told him that she loved him and that she wanted him to live because the truth was, Naresh being trained could easily kill him, which was not want she wanted. Deepak chuckled and kissed her back. Naresh walked away and was never seen for some four years, until something prompted him to wield the sword once again.

After returning, Naresh started living a quieter life. Aside from practicing martial arts, he spent a lot of time regretting the use of his skills for violence. Why? This was not exactly why he went on to train himself. While struggling to understand his emotions and their depth, Naresh found some peace when he started going to cinemas to watch new movies every week. For him, it was just a way to escape reality, until he became a fan of this new actress he watched in a new movie. He wanted to see her again, and developed feelings for her. Watching her videos and posts aside from the movies, Naresh went on to imagine as Sandhya, the imaginary girlfriend. So now, Sandhya had a new face and personality. Even though he heard she had a boyfriend and was going to marry him, Naresh only felt happy for her and prayed for her happiness.

It was until he learned she was supposedly murdered by her "boyfriend".

Naresh was left shattered even more when he learned the boyfriend was none other than Deepak. He felt anger rising and instantly felt the desire to kill Deepak, in spite of having sworn not to kill him. He went to his home city and found Sunanda living alone. He met her at her home, and found out that she was dumped by Deepak before he left for a hilly town. Sunanda told him about his whereabouts, along with the fact that Rajan accompanied him. When she asked him why he was searching for him now, Naresh told her, "*Vengeance*" and left her home. She didn't get it.

Seeing him walk away, Sunanda dialed Deepak's phone number and told him Naresh would be coming to kill him. Deepak initially refused to answer the call, but feared an emergency and hence answered it, to realize his enemy is still coming for him and won't spare him this time. This made him assign a group of assassins to kill him on his way to the hilly town. This is what happened until Naresh got rid of the assassins on the train and continued to stay aboard.

Back to present, Naresh has terrified all passengers on board. He is heading for the hilly town where Deepak, having heard nothing from the assassins, is waiting for him as well to fight off some of the strongest guards.

"A heart as sharp as a blade,
Leaves a scar never meant to fade.
It doesn't fear the consequences,
And is like its wielder unafraid."

CHAPTER FIVE

"A heart is on its way to war,
Blood is about to be shed.
For the sake of love and truth
Every enemy is about to be dead."

Naresh arrives in the hilly town via train and jumps out of the train before it stops at the platform. Picking up his bag, he books a taxi and orders to drive to Deepak's whereabouts as provided by Sunanda. On the way, Naresh stops for some breakfast. The sky is all cloudy, as if it could rain any moment. He wondered as to why Sunanda gave him Deepak's whereabouts so easily; does she really hate him a lot now? No idea. Naresh arrives at Deepak's house and asks a guard to meet with him. The guard tells him he is not there. Naresh decides to go and book a hotel first to stay there. He manages to find one such hotel and unwinds for some time. He begins talking to Sandhya while lying on the bed and looking outside the window, at the flowing river to be precise.

"I am here, baby. He has to pay this time. I'm no longer doing it for dad or his reputation. To clear his name without any evidence is as impossible as it sounds. I am here because you... you weren't supposed to die like that. Deepak must be visiting courts to clear his name, but ever since I heard he was involved, I developed the urge to kill him once and for all. He has been my enemy once, and is my enemy once again. And

this time I am not letting him walk away. The court might set him free in case of no evidence, but I will kill him and make sure he doesn't do it again. "

Deepak, on the other hand, is indeed busy visiting courts. Rajan, his father, is intrigued to learn that Atul's son Naresh killed his henchmen by chopping off their limbs. He is, however, also worried about the court's verdict. Until now, Deepak was merely a suspect, but anything could happen. Naresh too was unable to decide whether to kill him before after the verdict. He decides to wait for the verdict, since killing him before it could result in a good number of people thinking he might be innocent. In order to closely observe the scene, he enlists the help of Indu, a female reporter and his close friend. She agrees to help him, without realizing Naresh's true intentions.

With one day to go for the verdict, Naresh is getting restless and waiting for Indu's phone call or text regarding the case. Indu, on the other hand, is sitting in a park with her friend Vidya. Indu reveals she feels happier and more satisfied to realize Naresh is back in the town, even though she doesn't know how long he plans on staying. Vidya asks her if she still has feelings for him, and without any hesitation, Indu makes it clear that she still loves him. The two reporters keep chatting, until the verdict is finally delivered.

On the other hand, Naresh is getting restless waiting for the verdict and is about to turn on the television first, only to receive a call from Indu which he answers in a rush. Indu reveals Deepak has been allowed to walk free by the court. The actress was murdered, but it couldn't be proved that Deepak was involved. Hearing this, Naresh pauses for a while and asks Indu out on a date in a few hours after she got free from work. Indu happily agrees and the plan gets finalized. Naresh decides to interrogate Deepak in order to find out the truth. Deepak, on the other hand, returns home and his father happily welcomes him back. Deepak tells him he was always going to walk free, no matter what the evidence would say about him.

On the date, Naresh reveals his true intentions to Indu; he plans on using force to find out if Deepak actually killed the actress. Indu doesn't understand this and asks him if was somehow related to the actress. Naresh reveals he isn't, but instead of revealing how he saw her as his imaginary girlfriend, he points out that it was all due to a past incident that Naresh wants Deepak to suffer. Indu tells him any sort of vengeful action won't bring him peace. Naresh agrees but also tells her he isn't going to do it for vengeance precisely. *"Then what for?"* asks Indu. Naresh has no answer. He changes topic by asking her how she has been in the town and about her job. Indu tells him everything and then asks him about his life and job. Indu and Naresh then eat their meals, and begin walking in the park.

"You know... if we were actually dating, I would've taken you on a walk only." says Naresh. Indu smiles and asks him if he is considering doing so this time. Naresh tells her he is not prepared to fall in love yet, since his "trauma" had something to do with a girl he loved in the past. Indu feels slightly disappointed to know he fell for a girl other than her, but smiles and continues listening to his story. Indu starts to get teary-eyed listening to his story and gives him a hug. Naresh smiles and hugs her back before they continue walking and talking together. The sky is still replete with dark clouds, indicating it could rain anytime.

The next day, with the intention to interrogate Deepak, Naresh leaves early and armed with the sword, plans to break into his house. Deepak, on the other hand, is also waiting to surprise him by making him fight off five really strong guards skilled in martial arts and sword fighting. However, he plans on doing it away from his house and hence wants Naresh to get killed near the river so that his corpse too could be taken care of. With this in mind, he hands a recent photograph of Naresh (sent to him by Sunanda) to the five guards and plots to lure Naresh into a trap. The hunt for Naresh begins as the five men split throughout the town. Naresh is eventually discovered walking towards a taxi, and is followed, until the five of them regroup and stop his taxi near the river and railway line.

Naresh pays the driver and tells him to go. He exits the taxi with the sword in his hand. The five men draws their swords too. One of them contacts Deepak and lets him know Naresh has been found. Deepak feels excited to realize Naresh is going to have a tough time dealing with them. *"So you were sent by Deepak, right?"* says Naresh. One of them answers, *"Yes, Mr. Naresh"* and points the sword at him. Naresh smiles and soon all the five swords point at him. He realizes it's time for a battle. He tells himself this has to be the final time he would be using his skills for violence, and begins running towards the five with his sword pointed towards them. The five stand together with their swords, and prepare to clash with Naresh, who jumps and delivers the first blow with his sword.

"A heart is fighting a battle
It can never easily win
For between rage and madness
The line happens to be thin."

CHAPTER SIX

"A heart is wielding a sword
With the intention to slash its rival
For killing to live and living to kill
Is its only way of survival."

As the first blow is delivered by Naresh with his sword, the five swords clash with it and then scatter. Naresh recoils a bit and tries to slash their legs with a lower blow. All five, since they're working in sync, dodge the blow with finesse and deliver five minor cuts to Naresh's arm. Seeing he's bleeding slightly, Naresh smiles and proceeds to deliver a blow from behind. He runs towards them and jumps, trying to slash their backs as he falls behind them. However, all five dodge the movement and Naresh falls down. Now, the five men split and begin attacking him individually. One tries to stab Naresh but ends up impaling the road instead as Naresh dodges it, only to sense a sword coming for his neck from behind. Naresh dodges it a few seconds before it hits him, and he receives another minor cut, this time on his neck.

On the other hand, Deepak is sitting with Rajan and wondering what could potentially happen to Naresh: he could die or be left alive without a few limbs and so on. None of them think he can survive. That's how strong and challenging the five guards are.

Back to the fight, it has begun raining. Naresh is still continuing to get beaten, and it is evident from the injuries he has received on his chest. He continues swinging his sword throughout the battle, but only suffers more and more as it goes on to unfold. This makes him question his fate and what truly lies ahead for him. This is when he becomes distracted and receives a scar on his cheek. He asks them if they plan on killing him or capturing him alive. He doesn't get an answer. He lowers his head and smiles. The rain slows down, but continues to fall. Naresh gets up with the help of his sword and runs towards the group to attack them and slips. He gets up again and continues running, but gets kicked and stabbed by one of the five near the older chest injury. The guard slowly pulls out the sword and kicks him. Naresh falls into a puddle of water. He realizes he is indeed having a hard time defeating the five of them alone. It is then that he decides to play a new trick to buy himself time.

Naresh gets up, picks his sword and throws it down as a sign of surrender. He tells them he knows he will die if this kept going on. The five reveal they plan on killing him as per the orders. Naresh asks for a death wish to be fulfilled: he wants to know their stories about them and the women they love or have loved. The five initially don't comply, but Naresh pleads to be told the stories as his death wish, since he too was fighting this battle for the sake of love. Realizing they have time and an upper hand, they comply in spite of thinking it doesn't make any sense.

The first swordsman, Vilas, tells him how he met his wife Sneha.

Several years before becoming a skilled swordsman, Vilas used to be a shopkeeper. He used to deal with mental health issues and found it troublesome to keep up with the modern age. He was often scolded by his father for not doing his job perfectly, or for some other reason. Vilas had no other way to relieve himself, other than going on the terrace and looking at the sky. However, he used to stand a bit too closer to the edge of the terrace, and this caught Sneha's attention. She kept looking at him until he backed off a little. Vilas started noticing it after sometime and didn't understand why a girl would be interested in merely watching him stand. He would either back off for no reason, or just keep standing without moving an inch. One day, he finally found the courage to talk to her for the first time using hand gestures, except she was not there. He wondered where she might have gone and postponed the conversation.

When Sneha returned from a hospital, Vilas found out about it through the bandages on her arm. He decided to ask her out, and she happily joined him. Through their first conversation, Vilas found out Sneha used to think he was suicidal whenever he stood at the edge of the terrace. This made him chuckle a bit, before Sneha revealed she lost her brother who jumped off the terrace a few months ago. Vilas apologized and changed the topic. They had a good time together and one day, Vilas proposed to marry her. She reciprocated and they got married. He has two children in the present time.

"So... is that all? I mean, come on man! It can't be this ordinary! If something else happened, feel free to tell me since I'm going to die nonetheless." says Naresh. Vilas replies that there was nothing else to tell him or anyone else. Naresh lowers his head, before grabbing his sword and instantly stabbing Vilas by throwing it towards him. Vilas collapses, leaving everyone shocked. This time, Naresh begins laughing and violently pulls the sword out of Vilas's chest.

He orders the next one to tell his story as per their promise. The remaining four watch their comrade die painfully, and are forced to narrate their love stories one by one. Naresh's laughter only adds to their pain.

The second swordsman, named Nitin, begins telling his love story, while experiencing sadness and rage to see his comrade die like that. He realizes he and his teammates are in a situation where they have to do what Naresh wants them to do, especially because they have given their word.

Nitin worked at a gym. He was however addicted to social media, and was quieter than most people. As a student, he fell in love with a girl named Jyoti who was his classmate and it was love at first sight for him. He, however, turned red whenever anyone would talk about her. He kept looking at her from time to time without being addictive. He kept dropping hints for her, but it was as if she either didn't get it or didn't want to. He was still willing to loving her one-sided, and this cost him five years in which he barely interacted with her, and rather so much that he told his parents about her good grades and dancing skills but not her name.

Nitin suddenly stabs Naresh in the shoulder, back in present time, and kicks him away. Naresh is confused and enraged. He wants Nitin to continue telling his story, and reminds him of the word given. Nitin's comrades tell him to finish telling the story as they can kill Naresh together anyhow, at least in honor of the word Vilas gave Naresh. Nitin begins thinking about it and gets distracted. This gives Naresh an opportunity to briefly slash Nitin's arm with a pocket knife. Naresh points the sword towards his face and tells him to continue telling the story as he's in no mood to miss such an important and intriguing love story of a man who's not too different from him when it comes to interacting with girls.

"A heart is threatening other hearts,
To leave him alone or be killed.
It's not love that made him merciless,
Only hatred has left him so skilled."

CHAPTER SEVEN

"A heart wants to know what other hearts feel,
How similar or different it is from them.
It's not jealousy but also not admiration,
No one knows from where it gets to stem."

Nitin continues the storytelling.

Nitin decided to propose to Jyoti, but this "news" got leaked before he could make a move. Jyoti found out how he felt towards her, and ridiculed him in front of the class for that. Except teachers, almost the entire school found out that Nitin loved Jyoti. Nitin felt heartbroken since he didn't expect to be humiliated for merely falling in love, that too innocently. Plus, going through Jyoti's social media for the first time added more fuel to the fire. Her bio and posts left him enraged. He realized she was a toxic user who often hated on men in spite of having a boyfriend who was none other than her classmate. Realizing this, Nitin met her boyfriend Akash and asked him if he knew how toxic she was. Not having a presence on social media, Akash rebuffed him at first, but reading Jyoti's posts, he was left shattered. He couldn't believe it was the same girl he deeply loved. Nitin wished him luck for the future and left for home.

Few days after that, someone started cyberbullying him. Nitin didn't know who it was. He started feeling a lot of stress and began going out more than usual. He was unable to sit in front of his computer or mobile screen with social media apps. Every time he opened an app, it would be filled with filthy comments and posts injurious to one's mental health. Sometimes he would not use any apps and just try to watch a video or listen to a song instead, and would still being bombarded with stuff he wanted to avoid. He began wondering if his system had been hacked, and talks to an expert on this. He finds out his system is indeed hacked and someone who did this is now in full control unless Nitin is also controlling it. Nitin began wondering who it could be. Some rival? A troll? Who exactly? Nitin kept hiding from the toxicity of the social media, until a point where he decided he must not let the bully win. He continued spending time outside and with family, and it helped him deal with mental stress with ease.

When the bully showed up again, Nitin decided to not run away this time. He allowed the bully to speak or do anything, for it would ultimately have no effect on him. The bully started to get angrier than before and this could be seen in the replies. Nitin ridiculed the bully for being a "coward behind a screen" and threw in some profanity to hit the bully harder. The bully kept getting angrier and Nitin started feeling happy as if he was himself the bully now. The bully threatened to commit suicide if Nitin didn't stop, but somehow the latter had no sympathy for the bully and said, *"Do whatever you want, loser."* With this he stopped replying or commenting anything. When he looked at the clock after some 30 minutes, he realized there were no replies or comments from the bully and felt relieved. He ordered pizza as a sign of his victory and ate it all alone.

He went outside to meet up with his friends, only to learn of Jyoti's death. Nitin was shocked, learning of this and seeing her parents crying. Hearing them say she was quite addicted to the computer screen and often laughed loudly for no reason, Nitin feared she might have been the bully. He rushed to his house, and started messaging the bully to respond in some way. He even apologized and asked the bully to say something. No response came even after several hours. Nitin concluded the bully was none other than Jyoti, and he had somehow contributed to her death. However, he calmed himself down, opened the chat and deleted everything; this also meant the parts where he was the one bullied: the only thing that could be used in defense in case a case got filed against him. In order to avoid suspicion, he continued stepping outside and socializing with people. Nothing in his behavior could be seen with suspicion, and he was now used to socializing. He became used to this practice and slowly Jyoti's death faded away.

After that, he found another girl and in the present day, intends to propose to her. Listening to this story, Naresh lowers his head and starts to get enraged. Everyone is confused seeing him that way. Before Nitin could ask him anything, Naresh instantly stabs him with his sword and says, "*This is for driving my only sister to suicide.*" Everyone is shocked, including Nitin who tries to fight back, but all his blows are blocked by Naresh who pierces the sword deeper. Others try to intervene, but are successfully blocked by Naresh. Nitin, though stabbed, is unable to believe it. He asks Naresh if he is lying. Naresh tells him she was his only sister and he wanted revenge on the person responsible for her death. Nitin asks him if he knew it before the present confrontation, to which Naresh replies with a smile and a deeper piercing. He then violently pulls out the sword, leaving Nitin to collapse on the ground with a large splatter of blood. The other three and Naresh watch as Nitin dies slowly and uses gestures to call him closer and apologize, followed by his instant death. The remaining three are surprised once again as Naresh begins laughing.

He then proceeds to tell them he was obviously lying about the dead girl being his sister. This makes the three of them furious, and they start attacking him without wasting any time. Naresh smiles, and his confidence shows in his attacks. He blocks three swords with his own and kicks them while they are busy holding their swords. He chops off one's leg, while another loses an arm. Naresh fails to touch the third one, whose story he promises to listen to at the end. After some more sword-fighting, Naresh and the three guards realize there is enough distance between them. Naresh promises not to attack while listening to their stories. The guards decline his request. Naresh pleads them to keep their word in honor of their two dead comrades. He repeats his promise to not attack during the storytelling and picks the third out of five, telling him to tell his love story, before pointing out Nitin's story didn't really have a lot of "love" involved. Before telling his love story, the third guard named Raghunath, tells Naresh he will get to see a deadly attack after his story ends. Naresh welcomes the idea with a smile and tells him to begin.

It begins raining more than before, and blood from the corpses continues flowing and mixing into the river, changing its color red for some time.

"A heart did something unexpected,
Something dark and brutal to be precise.
Something cruel, something violent,

Something for which words won't suffice."

CHAPTER EIGHT

"A heart changed the way it beat,
And the way that beating sounded.
It however lost against the body's rebellion,
As it was from all sides surrounded."

Raghunath begins telling his love story.

A few years ago, Raghunath struggled to deal with anxiety. He had trouble talking to people, couldn't speak his heart out and happily sacrificed his own pleasures for those of others. He lived with his strict parents, who intended to make him a better person but their treatment turned him into a doubting person. He could barely trust anyone. Due to this, it wasn't him who made the move but a girl who loved his quiet and mysterious nature. He had no idea about how to deal with girls, especially when it came to romance, and while he felt this would leave the same girl unimpressed, that wasn't the case. The girl Megha introduced him to the outer world and helped him discover his passion for writing by sharing books with him.

Raghunath had decided to become a writer, and Megha helped him find a publisher as well. Amid all this, Raghunath developed feelings for her but the paranoia barely let him express any such feeling. Megha already loved him, but waited for him to tell her he loved her; it's not that she didn't know, she just wanted him to drum up the courage to express a feeling as pure as love. Raghunath one day expressed his love for her at college. She gave him his first kiss and a hug. Raghunath started opening up to her about his anxiety and how she should be prepared to handle him when he goes out of control a few times in the future. Megha said she knew it all, being a psychology student. However, he also told her about how paranoid he felt at times. He wanted to trust everyone, but just couldn't stop doubting anyone, including himself at times.

This had no negative effect on Megha, who was deeply in love with him. On the other hand, however, he started doubting his true feelings for her. Little did he know he also suffered from OCD, and this time it was about relationships. He also, even though he knew the truth, began doubting if Megha really loved him. This war inside his head between truth and a false reality began jeopardizing his mental health as time passed.

It took him over a year to realize he was suffering from OCD themed on relationships. He decided to talk to Megha about it, only to learn she had been engaged to a businessman. He couldn't understand what and how it happened. Her friends began pushing him away from her and this hurt Raghunath badly to the extent where he began sweating and his head started hurting. Megha realized this and told her friends to stop. When it got revealed that it was a prank, and even Megha was part of it, Raghunath became enraged and left the house. Megha tried calling him, but he kept rejecting her calls, only to answer later and tell her never to repeat these kinds of pranks due to his poor mental health. Megha apologized and invited him for her birthday. He agreed to come, unaware of what was to come next.

At the birthday party, Megha's brother Ravi arrived and got drunk. He made almost every guest drink some. Then Raghunath arrived with a gift for Megha. He met her and handed over the gift to her, and it was his first copy of his own book. Megha shook hands with him and hugged him.

"How about a kiss?" asked Raghunath.

"Stop it, not here!" replied Megha with a smile.

Here, Ravi noticed Raghunath standing alone as Megha left to meet some relatives. He called him and asked how he was related to Megha. Raghunath replied he was a close friend of hers and that she helped him publish his first book. Ravi asked him about the contents of the book, and the two talked for some 15 minutes. After that came the funny part as Ravi offered a drink to Raghunath. The latter declined, saying he didn't drink at all. Ravi, heavily drunk, still tried to make him drink and in the process grew aggressive. He initially tried to make him drink from a glass, and later tried to make him drink an entire bottle. Raghunath felt uncomfortable and pushed him away. Angry, Ravi grabbed the full bottle and smashed it on Raghunath's head. Everyone and everything stopped. Ravi wasn't done with it; he took the remaining piece of bottle and used it to slash Raghunath's face. Megha arrived and scolded Ravi for his violent behavior.

A bleeding Raghunath was in tears, which made Ravi laugh and tease him for being "weak". Megha arranged for a first-aid box and tended to his wounds. Raghunath was again struck by intrusive thoughts about his relationship with Megha, and eventually got up and left, after giving Megha a kiss on her cheek, much to the shock of everyone. Raghunath began driving fast and continued crying. He crashed near a hospital, luckily, and got admitted. The next day, after being discharged, he began driving away from the city. Within seconds, he realized he was being followed by someone. As he neared the city's borders, he stopped his bike. The person following him and his comrades stopped as well. Raghunath looked at who it was and began walking towards the bridge. Ravi and his comrades followed him to the bridge.

Ravi asked him why he kissed his sister the previous day. Raghunath replied he loved her and that she loved him too. This angered Ravi, who revealed he found about it last night itself and even hit Megha for it. Hearing this, Raghunath became enraged as he saw the comrades pull out their weapons. Raghunath ran towards them and a fight ensued. Ravi tried to hit Raghunath, but failed as the latter sought revenge by breaking a bottle on his head. He grabbed a metal pole thrown at him, and used it to beat up the comrades. Realizing Raghunath is indeed dangerous, they returned to their bikes and drew away. Only person remaining was Ravi, who got punched repeatedly in the face by Raghunath, and also received a heavy blow with the metal pole to his head. Raghunath soon realized he might have gone too far and killed him. As he approached Ravi to check if he's alive, he got stabbed in the knee by Ravi. Raghunath collapsed, but pulled out the knife violently and stabbed Ravi.

This is where he realized he really had gone too far. However, there was no way for him to fix it, and hence he kicked him down, in the river flowing under the bridge. He drove to the same hospital and got the required treatment. He returned home and was shivering. He couldn't believe he technically killed someone. Eventually, Ravi's absence began to be noticed. There were times Megha talked about it with Raghunath who'd somehow control his body language. One comrade who had followed Raghunath with

Ravi came up and told Megha Raghunath was involved in the situation. Megha, after a few days, asked Raghunath if he killed her brother, to which Raghunath began feeling anxious and broke down into tears. He hugged her and revealed it was not meant to happen. He then saw Ravi walking towards him, realizing he was not dead but only injured and away for a few days; His swimming skills saved him from dying. Raghunath instantly got away from Megha and began running, only to be stopped by Ravi, who then apologized for coming at him first. Raghunath also apologized for nearly killing him. Noting that none of them was drunk, their rivalry turned into friendship and has been so since then. Raghunath got married to Megha who is presently expected their first child.

Naresh remarks, "*That was violent yet pleasant. I just thought, by the way, that I should listen to the remaining love stories as well. Don't worry, I won't kill anyone of you before that, I promise.*"

"A heart chose to let other hearts beat,
Was it some clever scheme or trick?
Did it really want to hear them out,
Or wanted to kill them real quick?"

CHAPTER NINE

"A heart has begun sharpening its blade,
For a deadly war is about to begin.
Unless there are fighters involved,
How can someone get to lose or win?"

The fourth guard Abhishek began telling his love story.

Abhishek's love story began after he got married to Vandana. He never had an exposure towards the internet or modern gadgets, and all he learned came from his wife's support. He went on to feel love for her as time passed by. There was nothing else to say.

Abhishek quickly draws his sword and aims it at Naresh, who, slightly shocked, dodges the attack. "*Was that all? That was nothing!*" says Naresh and gets up. Drawing his sword, Naresh dodges the blow coming at him and throws his sword straight to Abhishek's chest, stabbing him severely. Abhishek's sword falls down and he too collapses, dying instantly. The fifth and last guard, named Jai, draws his sword. Naresh asks him if he's going to tell his love story or not, to which Jai responds by saying he likes a girl but is too shy to even go near her due to anxiety; that is all he will tell a stranger. Naresh asks him if he is willing to keep the word as kept by his comrades, to which he responds laughingly by saying he didn't consider them his comrades, but continued to act as if nothing happened so that he could see their attack strategies.

Hearing this, Naresh charges towards him, pulling his sword out of Abhishek's chest. The two swords clash and Naresh is the first to withdraw the sword and try to stab. However, all his moves are countered by Jai, who displays some extraordinary sword-fighting skills. Naresh faces a serious challenge fighting him off. He receives a scar on his face aside from a few slashes on his arm. Naresh starts to get angrier while Jai begins smiling. As raindrops begin pouring yet again, Naresh tries to deliver a lethal blow with his sword, but gets kicked instead. Jai starts laughing and challenges him to get up and finish the duel. Naresh struggles to grab his sword and fails.

He asks Jai to call a timeout before the duel resumes.

"Is it really even a duel anymore? At this point, it's just insanity." says Jai.

"I don't want to, but I agree. It's just pure insanity." replies Naresh.

During the break, Jai asks Naresh if he too has a story to tell. Naresh replies he has one but is unwilling to share it with anyone since it's embarrassing for him. Soon, the break ends as Jai gets up and points his sword at Naresh, who somehow gets up feeling weak and hurt. He holds his sword and points it at the sky. The rainfall continues and washes the blood-stained blade. Naresh immediately lowers it, points it at Jai and attacks first. Jai cleverly dodges his move and briefly slashes his back with his sword. Naresh collapses and touches his wound, before getting up and running towards Jai.

This time, he collapses midway.

Jai slowly approaches him to see if he's faking it. He realizes Naresh is unconscious and possibly exhausted from the excessive fighting. He calls Deepak for backup, which arrives in a few minutes and takes the two to Rajan's place, where Deepak is eagerly waiting to know the status of the mission. Jai steps out of the car and begins dragging Naresh out.

"The other four died, and this one survived with no injuries? Cool." says Deepak as he watches Naresh being dragged by his leg towards him. Jai throws Naresh in front of Rajan and Deepak. They ask if he is alive, and if yes, then why, since the orders were to execute him. Jai tells them he suffered multiple cuts across his body and suddenly dropped while coming to attack. He doesn't know what exactly happened but he just "died". Deepak begins laughing. Rajan and his henchmen begin laughing. Jai merely smiles.

Naresh suddenly gets up, pulls out a knife and stabs Deepak in the throat, before kicking him away. A henchman rushes to kill Naresh, only to get brutally punched in the face by the latter. The cup of coffee drops from Rajan's hand. Deepak lies on the ground, bleeding severely. With his blood covering the floor followed by some intense rainfall, Naresh kills the next few henchmen with his sword. Rajan becomes enraged and reaches out for his gun to shoot Naresh. However, he gets held with a sword on his neck by Jai, who had joined the four guards to kill Rajan as per the orders of a gangster. Rajan is surprised as Jai smiles and asks Naresh if he can kill him. Naresh tells him to wait until he finishes killing all the henchmen. More and more henchmen keep charging at Naresh, who, though wounded, continues fighting them off. With rain getting stronger by the second, Naresh begins to lose control of his blade.

As Rajan is held captive, Naresh suddenly remembers about Sunanda and becomes slightly distracted. His right hand, with which he is holding the sword, gets chopped off by one of the henchmen, and he collapses.

Jai is shocked too, and this gives Rajan a chance to escape captivity by first punching Jai on his chest, pushing and shooting him with his gun. Jai collapses to death. With Naresh collapsed and further stabbed in the thigh, Rajan points his gun at Naresh and asks him why he killed his son. Naresh begins speaking:

"I was initially concerned about the court's verdict, but after a point of time, I simply stopped caring. Your son wanted me dead, and I'm glad my pretending so helped him smile, even if for a few seconds. But I really wanted him dead this time. How do I explain this... A cold guy like you won't get it. It's... Oh God, what have I done? What have I become? I wanted justice for the actress I imagined and fantasized about as my imaginary girlfriend who was killed by your son. Why did I become a killer? I didn't just kill your son; I also killed the four swordsmen you sent to kill me. They had nothing to do with it...

...Except they had everything to do with it the moment they sided with you. I killed them because I wanted to, but didn't they want to kill me too? I did nothing wrong. I fell for a girl who tricked me, then I went on to see a beautiful actress... the most beautiful woman I had seen, to be precise. I was breathtaken. You can say that I was living in a bubble, but I loved it. And then your son had to ruin it. He killed her, didn't he?"

Rajan looks at him shocked, and tells him Deepak didn't do it; it was somebody else who killed the actress and framed Deepak. A detective hired by Rajan then arrives there, and tells him it was a girl named Sunanda who killed the actress and framed Deepak. She has left the city and is nowhere to be found. Both Rajan and Naresh are shocked. Naresh becomes enraged as he discovers Rajan is set to kill him with a point blank shot. Naresh smiles and apologizes, asking for a death wish fulfillment. Rajan allows him to fulfill it, following which Naresh looks at the Sun emerging from the clear sky, closes his eyes and prepares to die.

"A heart has a choice,
To say the truth or lie.
And either continuing to live
Or getting ready to die."

CHAPTER TEN

"A heart, in order to serve justice,
Made an important decision.
Nobody except the heart itself knows,
Whether or not it lacks precision."

However, Naresh is soon reminded of what was done to his father. He quickly opens his eyes and dodges the bullet by shifting to the opposite side of the gun. This is followed by a kick, and results in Rajan collapsing. Naresh holds him on gunpoint. Rajan tells him he can't shoot him since there was only one bullet in it and it got fired already. When Naresh pulls his sword towards him with his leg, Rajan begins laughing, telling Naresh he can possibly not fight him off since his hand, the right hand, has been chopped off. Listening to this, Naresh begins laughing too and tells him:

"Except... I am left-handed."

Naresh stabs Rajan with the sword and calls it vengeance in the name of Atul, his father. The detective puts his hands up, seeing Naresh hold a sword. Naresh tells him he won't kill him and only wants all the evidence he has found against Sunanda. The detective gives it to him, adding he himself is merely an investigator who works for a fee and hates violence. Naresh asks his name before he departs, and the detective reveals it to be *"Max Layer"*.

The death wish Naresh had asked for while Rajan was alive and about to shoot him, was a phone call to Indu; he told her where to find Sunanda's photograph and to run it across news channels in order to track her down. Except now she won't be doing it all alone. Naresh first goes to hospital and gets the necessary medication and treatments done. He then continues to meet Indu, who becomes teary-eyed seeing his right hand chopped off. Naresh consoles her and tells her it would all come to an end soon. All they need to do together now is to find out Sunanda. Her photograph is released in the media and the duo, including the cops, begins searching for her.

Naresh receives a call from Sunanda, who tearfully apologizes for leaving him. She sounds distressed and asks him to reconsider their past relationship before telling him her location and to come find her. Naresh informs Indu about this and the two board a train to the neighboring town Sunanda is presently in.

Arriving in the town, they first get a room at a hotel and then step outside to find out Sunanda. She texts Naresh the address to meet her, and the latter arrives there with Indu. Sunanda, who has been waiting to meet him since morning, is elated to see him, before she notices Indu with him. Sunanda asks him if he has considered trying one more time with her. Naresh tells her he doesn't love her anymore, and that he has fallen for another girl. Sunanda begins tearing up and apologizes for hurting him in the past. Naresh tells her he can't forgive her yet, for she is the reason behind the death of his imaginary girlfriend, and most importantly the actress: a real human being. Naresh asks Sunanda why she killed the actress, to which she responded by saying it was an accident. She didn't like her as an actor already, and hated her in person, but killing her was absolutely a mistake. When questioned about her relationship with Deepak, she reveals he loved the actress, and this made her, Sunanda, feel jealous.

She has more to add, but Naresh stops her midway. She begins telling him she loves him and that he should not let go of this golden chance since it is probably the first in his life that a girl is proposing to him instead of vice versa. She even asks him to forget the girl he loves. Naresh looks at his right arm and says something:

"So I lost my right hand for a girl like you? I guess it really wasn't worth it after all."

Sunanda starts feeling guilty. She reaches out for his arm, but is pushed back by Naresh, who tearfully tells her to stop acting and surrender to the police. Sunanda says she won't. *"Not even if there is evidence against you?"* asks Naresh. "*What evidence?*" asks Sunanda. Naresh tells her he has evidence against her handed over to him by a detective hired by Deepak's father. Indu is surprised and wonders if Naresh is making up a story. Naresh then comes up with an idea that should satisfy both sides. He confesses to her about killing Deepak, Rajan and his henchmen and decides to keep her secret about killing the actress a secret, as long she keeps his secret a secret.

Although a bit hesitant initially, Sunanda agrees. She promises to leave the town and never appear in front of him. She, however, tells him she can't stop loving him and that she would always wait for him to return to her someday. Naresh and Indu leave the rendezvous. Sunanda goes to her room at a hotel, teary-eyed and regretful. Naresh wonders why Sunanda left him earlier if she really loved him so much.

Naresh and Indu return to the hotel and turn on the television, only to discover Sunanda has surrendered herself to the cops and has nothing more to add besides the confession that she indeed killed the actress. Naresh doesn't understand her again, and wonders if it's better this way. He smiles, feeling the poor actress's soul might finally find some peace.

Naresh and Indu board the returning train the next day. Naresh is looking at his phone, and notices Indu looking at a couple holding hands. As the horn blows, Naresh puts down his phone and raises his left hand. Indu looks at him. Naresh makes a poker face and stares at her, only to smile and signal her to hold his hand. Indu smiles and holds the hand. Her smile grows bigger when Naresh kisses her hand and finally succeeds in saying this to a girl for the first time:

"I love you."

"A heart finally found the one,
With which it always wanted to beat.
The day it found love was the day,
It won and didn't face defeat."

Bonus Poem: Petrified

The path I chose to find you
Finally led me to question and decide
Whether meeting you would soften my soul
Or forever leave me petrified.
There were other ways to meet you
Sadly none worked in my case
Was it an indication that
I'd be left with a sad face?
No, that could never happen
Whether I got to live or died
There's no way your love
Could leave me petrified.

Bonus Poem: Don't Leave Me

It's not that I have never been
Left alone before
It's just that when you leave
I feel lonely some more
I want to hold your hand
Your beauty I want to adore
Just stay with me now
Don't leave me like before
We have lots of time
For each other in store
I plead you to stay with me
Don't leave me like before.

9 798885 915304

Printed by Libri Plureos GmbH in Hamburg, Germany